Snowplows

Quinn M. Arnold

CREATIVE EDUCATION • CREATIVE PAPERBACKS

seedlings

Published by Creative Education and Creative Paperbacks
P.O. Box 227, Mankato, Minnesota 56002
Creative Education and Creative Paperbacks are imprints of
The Creative Company
www.thecreativecompany.us

Design by Ellen Huber; production by Dana Cheit
Art direction by Rita Marshall
Printed in the United States of America

Photographs by Dreamstime (Bambulla), iStockphoto
(BanksPhotos, CHBD, cweimer4, dagsy10, gmattrichard, Theresa
Granger, Groomee, invisiblepower, JonathanLesage, kudou, ollo,
santosha, Sjo, tamaw, valio84sl, Jorge Villalba, ZargonDesign),
Shutterstock (aapsky, mariakraynova, Petite usagi)

Library of Congress Cataloging-in-Publication Data
Names: Arnold, Quinn M., author.
Title: Snowplows / Quinn M. Arnold.
Series: Seedlings.
Includes bibliographical references and index.
Summary: A kindergarten-level introduction to snowplows,
covering their purpose, parts, community role, and such
defining features as their plow blades.
Identifiers: ISBN 978-1-64026-071-9 (hardcover) /
ISBN 978-1-62832-659-8 (pbk) / ISBN 978-1-64000-187-9 (eBook)

This title has been submitted for CIP processing under LCCN
2018939106.

CCSS: RI.K.1, 2, 3, 4, 5, 6, 7; RI.1.1, 2, 3, 4, 5, 6, 7; RF.K.1, 3; RF.1.1

First Edition HC 9 8 7 6 5 4 3 2 1
First Edition PBK 9 8 7 6 5 4 3 2 1

TABLE OF CONTENTS

Hello, Snowplows! 4

Community Clearers 6

Colors and Lights 9

Spreading Salt and Sand 10

Snowplow Drivers 13

Bad-Weather Driving 14

What Do Snowplows Do? 16

Goodbye, Snowplows! 19

Picture a Snowplow 20

Words to Know 22

Read More 23

Websites 23

Index 24

Hello, snowplows!

Snowplows clear roads and parking lots.

Their big blades push snow.

Most snowplows
are orange or
yellow. These
big trucks have
flashing lights.

Some have a
scraper under
the truck.

Snowplow hoppers may hold salt or sand. They spread it over the road.

Salt melts ice.
Sand helps tires
grip the road.

A snowplow driver sits in the cab.

The driver lowers the blade when it is time to plow.

Bad weather
does not stop
a snowplow.

It has 10 big wheels.
The truck moves slowly
as it plows.

Snowplows push snow off streets. They drop salt or sand.

They keep community roads clear.

Goodbye, snowplows!

Picture a Snowplow

flashing lights

mirror

cab

tire

salt

hopper

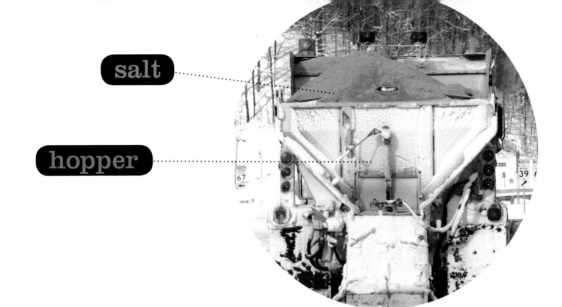

exhaust pipe

plow blade

cab: the front part of a truck

hoppers: the back parts of big trucks; hoppers hold loose materials

scraper: a smaller blade used to remove ice

Read More

Meister, Cari. *Snowplows.*
Minneapolis: Jump!, 2017.

Pettiford, Rebecca. *Snowplows.*
Minneapolis: Bellwether Media, 2018.

Websites

Reading Confetti: 3-D Shape Snowplow
http://www.readingconfetti.com/2013/01/3-d-shape-snowplow
-craft-for-boys.html
Complete the craft to make a snowplow.

YouTube: Mighty Machines: In the Snowstorm
https://www.youtube.com/watch?v=zI4E1JTN0GA
Watch a video about machines that help clear snow after a storm.

Note: Every effort has been made to ensure that the websites listed above are suitable for children, that they have educational value, and that they contain no inappropriate material. However, because of the nature of the Internet, it is impossible to guarantee that these sites will remain active indefinitely or that their contents will not be altered.

23

Index

blades **7, 13**

cabs **13**

colors **9**

drivers **13**

hoppers **10**

lights **9**

roads **6, 10, 11, 16, 17**

salt **10, 11, 16**

sand **10, 11, 16**

scrapers **9**

wheels **15**